SCHOLASTIC
Phonics

Nap, Sid!

Can you spot the cat on 4 pages?

Published in the UK by Scholastic Education, 2021
Book End, Range Road, Witney, Oxfordshire, OX29 0YD
Scholastic Ireland, 89E Lagan Road, Dublin Industrial Estate, Glasnevin, Dublin, D11 HP5F

www.scholastic.co.uk

1 2 3 4 5 6 7 8 9 1 2 3 4 5 6 7 8 9 0

Printed by Ashford Colour Press
Paper made from wood grown in sustainable forests and other controlled sources.

A CIP catalogue record for this book is available from the British Library.

ISBN 978-0702-30864-2

Author
Catherine Baker

Editorial team
Rachel Morgan, Tracy Kewley, Liz Evans

Design team
Dipa Mistry, We Are Grace

Illustrations
Kevin Payne

It is a mat.
Sid

The mat is in.

Tip it in, Sam.

tip

Nap in it, Sid!

Retell the story

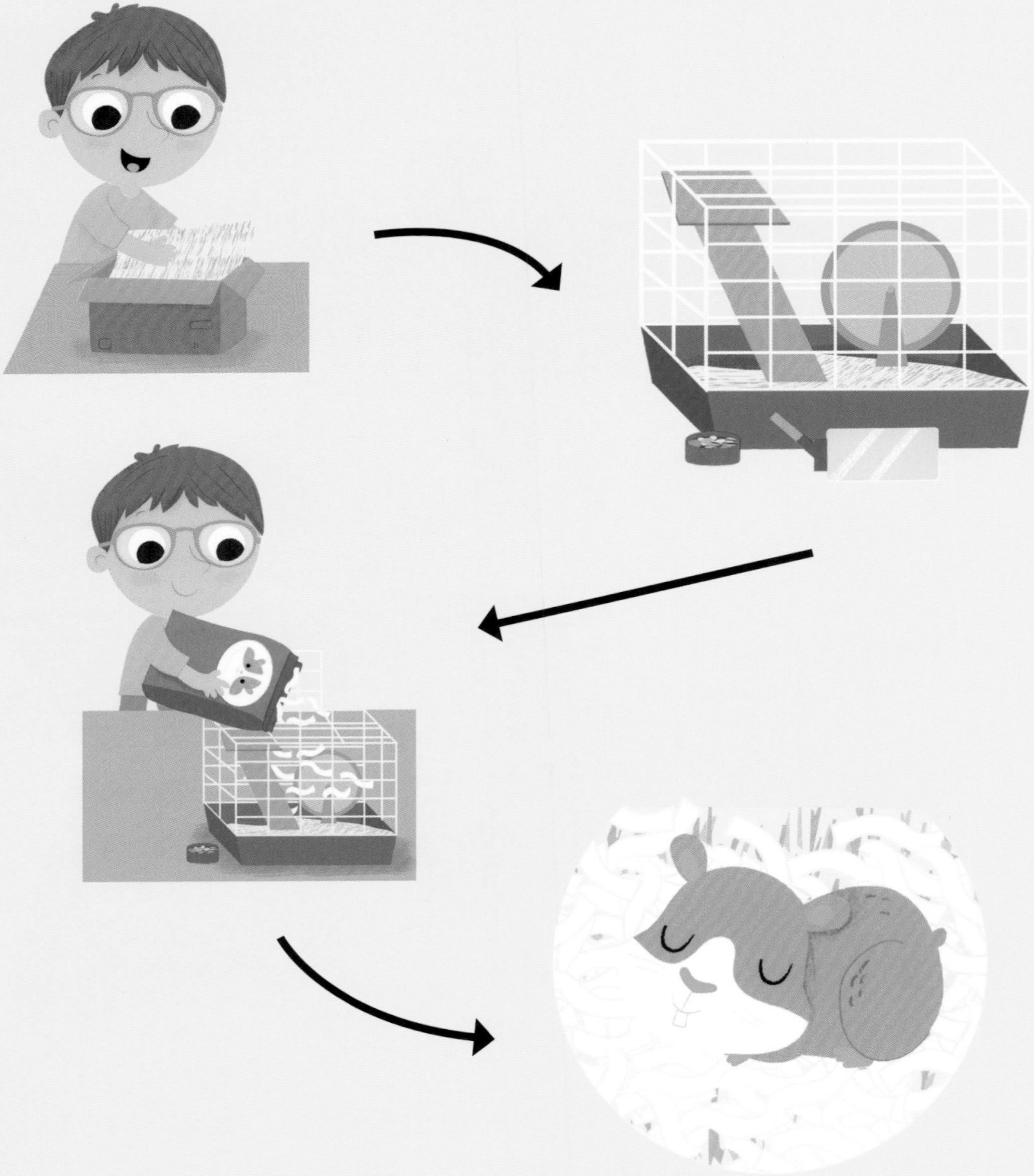